# The
# Fifteenth
# Pelican

# The
# Fifteenth
# Pelican

## by Tere Ríos

*Illustrations by Arthur King, O.M.I.*

*Doubleday & Company, Inc., Garden City, New York*

## 1965

*All of the characters in this book*
*are fictitious,*
*and any resemblance*
*to actual persons,*
*living or dead,*
*is purely coincidental.*

Library of Congress Catalog Card Number 65–19885
Copyright © 1965 by Tere Ríos
All Rights Reserved
Printed in the United States of America
First Edition

FOR THE ROCK
and the chicken and sugar
people of NamCan.

# *One*

San Juan is on a high cliff on an island, and across it sweeps the trade wind of the Spanish Main. At thirty miles per hour it romps in through the windows and puffs off bureau scarves, catches the edges of the bedspreads and whips them off; and what with the gusts as strong as fifty miles per hour, by the end of any day everything blowable in a house is piled up against the opposite walls.

It was this wind that one day met Sister Bertrille coming around a corner, fresh from the U.S.A.

Of all the nuns in all the world, Sister Bertrille was probably the smallest. She had dark eyes, brows like gull wings, a small nose with one freckle; and she hurried all the time—partly to keep up with all the big people surrounding her, and partly because she was just a natural-born hurrier.

At the top of the highest hill in San Juan is the Convento San Tanco, where the Daughters of Charity, their folded cornettes like big white birds in flight, scoot and scurry among the windy colonnades, taking care of their thirteen Old People and twenty-three Children.

Sister Plácido was the sister in charge. (They called her the Sister Servant, but nobody really believed *that*.) Sister Plácido had come to this gay, warm, sunny island long ago, but such was her strength of character that she had retained every inch of her Spanishness; she was *very* everything she was: very tall, very thin, very serious, very strict, and very good at everything she did. She had Definite Ideas on everything, most of them beginning with, *Sisters don't*. Besides which, she was a Disciplinarian, believing that Comportment Conquers Comfort.

So it was the worst shock in Sister Plácido's twenty years as a Sister Servant when she and Sister Sixto went to meet the new American Sister, Sister Bertrille, at the ship. Sister Sixto always went with Sister Plácido to meet ships, because Sister Sixto was large and strong, though a bit giddy, and she could carry a great deal of luggage without gasping.

Little Sister Bertrille could hardly see over the ship's rail, but she waved gaily at the two who had come to meet her. She knew who they were because they both wore blue dresses and great big white bonnets called cornettes. They didn't wave back, so she called to them and waved again.

*That* was bad enough! (Spanish Sisters never wave at people. They tuck their hands in their sleeves and lower their eyes and indicate a nod. And that's *all*.)

But now Sister Bertrille ran to the gangplank, ran back for her things, let five men pick them up for her,

ran back down, and halfway to the dock, she turned and waved a warm, bright good-by to the sailors who had brought her on their ship.

Sister Sixto gasped.

Sister Plácido froze. Solid.

Right up to the two nuns Sister Bertrille skipped, followed by five beaming men carrying her bag, her books, her umbrella, and a huge basket of fruit with an orange satin bow on top.

She skidded to a stop before the two Spanish Sisters, tucked her hands in her sleeves, lowered her eyes, and almost looked like a Spanish Sister, except that there was clearly an invisible sparkle and twinkle in the air about her whole blue-clad person that was pure American. This comes, some theorists say, from vitamins, ice skating, braces on the teeth, dancing lessons, and liberal doses of free air.

Sister Plácido was still speechless.

Sister Sixto, eyes lowered, leaned forward just as Sister Bertrille turned away to thank the men who were putting her luggage down, and when she turned back they were nose to nose.

"Sister Plácido can't *speak*," Sister Sixto whispered.

"Oh?" Sister Bertrille raised her voice as though Sister had said that Sister was deaf. "I'M SISTER BERTRILLE!" she said, as if they didn't know.

"We *know*," Sister Sixto whimpered. "What I meant to say was, Sister can't speak because Spanish Sisters *never*"—she could hardly say the words— "*wave at sailors.*"

"Oh," said Sister Bertrille; then: "Oh-oh." She

lowered her eyes before Sister Plácido and somehow
the freckle on her nose dimmed and faded. "I beg
your pardon, Sister. You see, we all came to be such
great friends on the voyage. Each night we sat on
deck and sang songs, and when it rained, we played
cards—"

There was a violent, unmoving *agitation* in Sister
Sixto and, too late, Sister Bertrille realized that of
course, if Spanish Sisters don't *wave* at sailors, they
would hardly play cards with them. She could find
nothing to say.

Sister Sixto heaved her weight around and picked
up Sister Bertrille's suitcase and books, one under
each arm.

Sister Bertrille picked up her umbrella and took
measure of the basket of fruit, which was bigger than
she. It was a wistful glance she gave it, because her
cousin Bernie the Bartender had given it to her, and
she had a feeling that the holy poverty of Spanish
Sisters wouldn't let them go in for things like im-
ported jellies and cheeses, smoked oysters and caviar,
fruit so beautiful it looked fake and all with an orange
satin bow on top. She herself liked the red caviar
best; she liked to pop it between her teeth.

She murmured, without much hope, "My
cousin . . ."

Sister Plácido was looking at the fruit. She found
her voice, and it was thin, cool, remote. She talked
to herself, almost. "Oh! Pears . . . apples . . .
peaches: *cold* country fruit! Oh, those lovely frosty
mornings in the Pyrenees . . ."

Sister Bertrille hoped that maybe things wouldn't be so bad after all. "Sister . . . may we accept it?"

Sister Plácido left her childhood in the Pyrenees and snapped back to the present. "Our Old Ones, our Children . . . they have never seen such things. We shall have a combined geography lesson and class in etiquette: a tea. Sister—you speak Spanish?" She accepted the nod, bent and picked up the elaborate wicker handle and waited for Sister Bertrille to heft the other side. Since Sister Plácido was very tall and Sister Bertrille very small, the basket had a sharp list to starboard, but it cleared the ground, and they started off behind Sister Sixto, who manfully bore the full burden of books and bag across the busy dock street.

Several people offered to help Sister Sixto, but she grimly shook her head and went on, saying to them that she was getting grace.

One frail old man said in answer, "Share me some of that grace, then, my sister," and took the bag from her without waiting for her permission.

Then a young man took the books, a policeman took the fruit basket, and a scrawny, almost-naked boy took the umbrella and danced ahead, wielding it like a sword of honor.

Sister Bertrille, embarrassed by the whole wildly colorful procession, glanced at her superior to see how she (who went speechless at waving at sailors) was taking it.

Sister Plácido sailed on in aloof majesty, accepting calmly not only the pre-procession carrying the

luggage but also the curious who followed along behind, remarking on Sister Bertrille's appearance. She
accepted the whole thing as though it were a not-
quite-good mural. No, more than that; because when
someone called out to her from the curb (the parade took up the full width of the narrow cobbled
street) and asked a blessing she nodded graciously
and moved on like a mitered abbess.

"*Blessing?*" Sister Bertrille asked.

"I pray God gives it."

"Oh."

And the remarks went on. Sister Bertrille didn't
know that this was a custom, a polite way of letting
a person know that she doesn't pass unnoticed.

"It's the new nun for the *pobres* at San Tanco."

"Pretty, eh? But she's hardly bigger than the little
ones she'll have to teach."

"You'd hardly know she's an *americanita* by those
handsome dark eyes."

"Sure you can. She walks like a boy, see? No wig-
gle."

Sister Bertrille stopped in her tracks. It was too
much! Insulting nuns, indeed! But nobody meant to
insult her; the remarks were just to let her know they
saw her without actually speaking *to* her, in case she
wasn't allowed.

The parade behind her had halted, and Sister Superior had moved on, leaving her alone with the remarks. She ran to catch up, up a long, steep hill.
They crossed a level street, then another long hill.

"As I was saying," Sister Plácido went on, as

though nothing had happened between the time they had picked up the fruit basket and here, almost at the top of the city, "we shall have a geography-tea, an English tea; but we shall serve coffee, since it is a product of the island. And you, Sister, shall serve each delicacy, giving its history and a short lecture on the country of its origin."

Sister Bertrille gasped. The freckle on her nose turned pale. She didn't know *what* half the things were, much less where they came from. What *was* caviar? Once she had heard a song about it, but she didn't think Sister would appreciate that. Besides, she comforted herself, it would probably suffer in translation. But why was some caviar red and some black? And how about *pâté de foie gras?* She imagined herself saying, "A sort of liverish peanut butter . . . ," but would Puerto Rican children know what peanut butter was?

Sister Plácido must have read her mind. "We have quite a good library," she said, indicating that what Sister Bertrille didn't know she could look up.

They passed a grocery store open to the sun, and Sister bowed to the proprietor and said graciously, "Don Scarpo . . . ," and passed on before his sweeping bow.

And right there, in the hot yellow sunlight, on a windy corner at the top of San Juan, with skinny Don Scarpo looking on from the doorway of his store, was where it happened for the first time.

The wind had been buffeting them about all the time, snapping their skirts like flags, puffing up their

sleeves, rattling their stiff-starched white bonnets.
But that was only the steady wind; they hadn't met
a gust yet. But here, at the Convento San Tanco
corner, a fifty-mile-an-hour gust hit them.

People who know about airplanes and why they
stay up say that if *lift* + *thrust* is greater than *load* +
*drag*, a thing will fly.

Sister Bertrille's wide white cornette, folded like a
paper airplane with the point at the front, was a perfect airfoil (an airfoil is anything like a wing that
gives *lift*); she was running to keep up, which gave
her *thrust*; her tiny body was very little *load*, and
practically no *drag*.

So when she skipped up over the highest hill in
San Juan and turned the corner and lifted her head
and ran a bit to catch up, that gust lifted her right
into the air.

Astonished, she threw her arms out, and her wide
sleeves made *more* airfoil. She hovered there, about
a foot off the ground, for fully thirty seconds.

Then she looked *down*, which angled her cornette
down; she threw her arms *up*. Her airfoils angled so
sharply, she shot into a steep glide and landed with
a bucking skid that looked like a stumble to anyone
who wasn't watching carefully—and that was everyone but Don Scarpo, who watched with interest, but
no comment.

Sister Plácido hadn't seen her take off and hover,
so when she stumbled beside her, she didn't even
turn her head, but said frostily out of the corner of
her mouth without moving her lips (in the same way

that soldiers on parade and prisoners in line talk to each other, so no one will see that they're talking) to Sister Bertrille, "Less haste, more grace, Sister."

Sister Bertrille recovered her poise and her breath at the same time.

"Yes, Sister," she murmured, and slunk along close to the wall of the convent, where the wind seemed to blow things *downward.*

# *Two*

The building of the Convent of San Tanco was a block square and three stories high, and it ran in colonnaded balconies all around a cobbled patio planted with flowers and set about with benches. The kitchen, refectory, classrooms, offices, and parlors were on the first floor; the Children slept on the city side of the second floor, and the Old Ones on the ocean side; on the third floor was the convent, and the roof.

Spanish houses have flat roofs, so hurricanes can't catch under eaves and rip them off. And these roofs have low walls around them so that the people won't fall off, because the people *use* their roofs: they have gardens up there (the Sisters of San Tanco grew herbs and small vegetables); they exercise and rest in the sun up there; and at night they watch the glorious skies. The Sisters also hung their laundry out up there, and that was where Sister Bertrille was the next time it happened.

She was alone on the roof. It was early on a Saturday morning, when the breeze was strong from across the sea, a blustery, blowy day, even for San Juan.

One minute, she was peacefully pinning a sheet to the clothesline; and the next, she was floating above the sheet, her nose with one freckle pointed into the wind, her habit flapping at her ankles, and she was holding onto the clothesline for dear life.

The only person who saw her was Don Scarpo, standing in the doorway of his store across the street. He gazed up meditatively at the nun flapping from the clothesline on the roof, smoothed his thick wavy mustache, and watched with interest.

"Help," she said weakly, but the wind blew the word right back into her mouth and she choked on it and almost let go.

No one was going to hear her, she knew that, with a wildly pounding heart. Her hands hurt, her shoulders ached—she would have to get down herself. How had she got down, there in the street? By ducking her head. It was her only chance.

She waited for a gust to die down, and in the lull, she ducked her head and pulled with her arms with all her might—and hit the roof in a magnificent nose dive: a pancake landing that skinned her nose and chin.

Sister Sixto, the big and strong one, had come up the steps just at that moment, and she took a heroic flying leap and landed on top of Sister Bertrille, weighting her down.

They lay there for quite a while, Sister Bertrille recovering from the two impacts, Sister Sixto trying not to believe what she had seen.

Finally Sister Sixto lifted her head.

Sister Bertrille groaned.

"Sister," Sister Sixto said apologetically, "I don't like to pry into your private affairs—but—were you being blown about, or were you . . . *flying?*"

Sister Bertrille could hardly breathe with all that weight on top of her. She said through her teeth (Sister Sixto's elbow was sticking into her throat and holding her jaw shut), "A little of bose, I sink."

Sister Sixto eased up, keeping one strong arm firmly around Sister Bertrille, and they crept to the sheltered lee of the guard wall.

"I'm sorry to leap on you like that, but I really thought you were being blown away."

Sister Bertrille tenderly touched her chin where it had been scraped raw. "I was, I think."

"Well," said Sister Sixto, "if you'll accept a little advice from a heavier person, if I were you I wouldn't come up here again without me to hold you down."

"Oh, I wouldn't!" Sister Bertrille said fervently.

They meditated upon that for a moment; then Sister Bertrille patted her scraped nose with her handkerchief and looked at the pink stain ruefully and said in a small, still voice that was almost lost in the sound of the sea and the wind (except that Sister Sixto had been expecting it, and heard what she expected to hear), "I suppose now we'll have to tell Sister Plácido."

Sister Sixto took the handkerchief and nipped a bit of gravel out of the nose wound. "I don't know," she said doubtfully. "Sister Plácido had a heart attack last year."

Sister Bertrille was torn between proper sorrow for another's pain and delight that maybe it wouldn't be *right* for them to tell Sister Plácido after all. "I didn't know," she said.

"Coronary occlusion," Sister Sixto said. "I don't know if—well, I did think she was about to have another attack that day that you . . ." She let her voice trail off in delicate discretion.

". . . waved at sailors." Sister Bertrille sighed. "I know."

They meditated some more, sitting in the lee of the wall.

Finally Sister Sixto broke the silence. "I shall take it upon myself. After all, I am familiar with the situation and you are not. We shall not tell Sister." And at the sheer joy that flooded Sister Bertrille's dark eyes she added hastily, "*But,* please, Sister, don't go out when it's windy, or if you have to, please take me?"

"Oh, yes! I will!" Sister Bertrille leaped up, was buffeted about for a moment, but Sister Sixto had a firm grip on her ankles, so they went safely below to the third, then the second, then the first gallery, and on to prepare the International Tea, with Lectures by Sister Bertrille.

The tea was a lovely success. Only two of the Old Ones and three of the babies fell asleep, and the others were all much enlightened and filled by the contents of Cousin Bernie's fruit basket.

Sister Plácido even weakened and ate a peach: she ate it right down to the dry red stone, licked each finger genteelly, then sighed, and smiled at Sister Bertrille, and said, "You have brought me much happiness today."

Sister Bertrille tried to smile back but she kept thinking of how much unhappiness she could bring Sister if she thought that one of her Sisters was flying about above the convent.

The next day Sister Bertrille went across the street to Don Scarpo's store to buy some garlic. She herself would never have given those Old Ones garlic: she'd have given them baby food and vitamins and maybe hormones—but garlic was what they liked, and garlic was what Sister Plácido had said they might have. So, in holy obedience, across the street she went and bought garlic.

Don Scarpo's silky mustache dwarfed his skinny self and it shimmered as he spoke, telling her good morning, the price of the rope of garlic, making change; but all the time his eyes watched her as though he were waiting for her to take off and zoom out of there a bit above the ground. But he didn't say a thing. That wasn't his way. If a Sister wanted to fly, that was her business. There were days when even the birds walked, and a Sister might want to walk more often than that. Though if it were he, and he were *able* to fly, he wouldn't have spent much time on the ground. So Don Scarpo simply transacted his business with her, wished her another good morn-

ing, and wished that she would fly, but he didn't mention it. That wouldn't have been polite.

He watched her go out the door, one hand on the wall, weighted only slightly by the rope of garlic over her shoulder. He had no trouble telling the Sisters apart: Sister Plácido was tall and thin, Sister Sixto was equally tall, but broad as a wall; Sister Cook—well, one could smell Sister Cook and Sister Laundress before they came in: the wind would puff a gust laden with garlic, onions, saffron, thyme, basil —and one knew that Sister Cook was coming; or the smell of soap and bleach and starch—and Sister Laundress was not very far behind.

Funny things they were, all of them, as he considered them from the lofty heights of his male point of view. Their bonnets were unwieldy, their clothing heavy but not ungraceful, being that pretty blue color—yet they all asked and took his advice; he often had to recommend to them what to buy and when to buy it . . . And this new one, Sister Bertrille. . . . The name sounded like a name for a bird—and from what he had seen, it fit.

Don Scarpo was not a man to argue with the Almighty: if He saw fit to make bumblebees fly, and Lord knew *they* were clumsy enough—and how about the big, awkward brown pelicans? So if bumblebees and pelicans, why not a tiny Sister?

Don Scarpo went back to business, and Sister went back to the convent with her rope of garlic, suffering only a mild bumping about as she turned the corner from Calle Monjas to Calle Sol.

That afternoon she was to take her little Children
to the beach. They couldn't swim, because of the
sharks and barracuda, but they could play in the
sand, gather shells, wade a bit, chase gulls and feed
them, dig after the little crabs that always get away—
oh, Saturday afternoons at the beach were lovely for
the little ones, and Sister Bertrille would enjoy it with
them, and for them.

Sister and the seven five-year-olds crossed the
street, made their way through a break in the ancient
city wall, then clambered down a mass of rubble to
a tiny beach in the shadow of Fortress San Cristóbal.

The Children played, and Sister watched them . . .
and helped them with the shell-gathering . . . and toward evening, when "To the Colors" and "Retreat"
sounded from the battlements of the old fortress, Sister gathered the Children around her to listen to the
sweet clear notes of the bugle, then sat down to tell
them just one more story before time to go home.

"What shall the story be about?" she asked them.

Perico looked up at the sky. "Pelicans."

"Pelicans!" An arm about each of two Children,
three mites in her lap, the other two crowded close,
Sister looked up at a long, gliding line of pelicans
soaring above them.

She had seen pelicans in the zoo at home, and on
the ground, in a cage, they were awkward, comic, ugly
creatures. But here, in their own turquoise sky, their
wings spread wide, they were beautiful. The big,
graceful brown birds sailed high above the edge
of the water, following the line of the beach, in per-

fect single file, one behind the other. They rose and fell with the motion of the drafts of air, and hardly moved their wings at all. Like sailplanes, their wings spread like giant fans; motionless, they rode the air currents. Only the leader, occasionally having made a misjudgment about where the air was moving, would flap his wings and lazily pull the whole line of fourteen pelicans along after him as he swam over to where the air would be more buoyant.

"It looks so *easy*." Sister sighed.

"It is," Perico said. "For a pelican."

So she laughed and told them a story about a pelican who took too much food in his mouth and had to walk until he learned to eat like a pelican instead of a pig.

# Three

Sister Bertrille began to dream of flying. All the sensations of glorious flight were there: soaring, dipping, climbing, diving, circling, slipping—each and all she experienced in dreams at night, while during the day she woke little people up and washed and combed them and taught them in kindergarten and took them for walks and loved them and scolded them just like a real mother. And she taught them their manners.

Sister Plácido had come upon her while she was teaching the Children American table manners.

All that switching about of knife and fork, Sister Plácido said, seemed pretty much to her like a drummer boy showing off with extra trills and flourishes. Not really necessary to the music, although rather decorative.

The Sisters stood off to one side of the refectory, talking through unmoving lips, so that neither the Children nor the Old Ones could hear.

"But Sister," Sister Bertrille said, "*I* don't know how to eat European style."

"You mean, all this affectedness is *natural* to you?"

Sister Bertrille didn't know how to say that affectedness isn't affected if it's what you grew up with and all that you know, without seeming to be impudent, which isn't the thing to seem in any convent, if that's where you want to spend the rest of your life.

Sister Plácido was waiting for an answer, so Sister Bertrille took refuge in the indirect. "This is the American way of eating." And when Sister looked incredulous, she nodded emphatically. "*Everybody* in America eats like that."

Sister Plácido's eyebrows disappeared under her cornette. "Sister," she said, "I have no reason whatsoever to doubt your word, when you say that everyone in America eats like that. On the other hand, I cannot bring myself to approve all this flourishing of the instruments; it seems a rather peasantish attempt at elegance. However, since these are American Children . . ."

That was all she said. But Sister Bertrille understood that permission had been given to teach the Children to eat American style, switching the knife and fork from hand to hand with each cut, and eating with the fork turned up like a spoon. It was just that Sister Plácido couldn't bring herself to say the actual words.

"Yes, Sister. Thank you, Sister." Sister Bertrille moved to go back to her charges, but Sister Plácido's voice halted her.

"Sister."

Sister Bertrille halted.

"I think that the Old Ones should be allowed to live out their lives in harmony and comfort."

"Yes, Sister."

Then, she was dismissed with a nod and went back to the Children to teach them to hold the fork like a pencil, to exchange it for the knife at each cut; and she knew that she was to leave the Old Ones alone, and not try to turn them from their own customs.

Her Children's problems kept her too busy to worry about anything else, anyway. For instance, "show and tell," a necessary part of the kindergarten day: what is there to show and tell about, when all live together in one room, all go together to everything? In "show and tell" in a regular school, each child brings something from his own home, shows it to the class, and tells about it. But here everyone had the same home. Everyone knew about everything in it.

Next year her seven kindergartners would be moved to the orphanage for big Children and would start in the first grade—and they should be ready for first-grade teaching methods. It was a poor home that sent a child to school too bewildered by all the strangeness to be able to function in the new environment.

And in first grade, she knew, there was always "show and tell."

She mentioned this problem to Don Scarpo. She didn't know why, but the task of running to his store each day had fallen to her. He smoothed his silky mustache and said, "Let me think about this."

And he did, while Sister stood first on one foot and then on the other, and finally he said, "How many Children?"

"Seven."

He reached into the candy case and came up with seven pieces of candy: one caramel, one chocolate kiss, one orange gumdrop, one piece of nougat, one piece of peppermint, one licorice stick, and one sour-ball.

He passed them over to her. "When you kiss them good night—" He stopped, looked his question. "You *do* kiss them?"

"Oh, yes. And tuck them in tight. And listen a while, because sometimes when it's dark they need to talk."

"Good, then. This is their homework, clear? They must eat it before sleeping, then think about the taste all night, and in the morning each must describe his candy to the class and then let the class ask questions and guess what kind of candy it was."

"Oh, Don Scarpo, thank you!" For one night, she thought, she would pretend that the Rules of Dental Health were not there. What fun would a special piece of candy be if they had to jump up out of their cozy beds and brush their teeth?

Then she thought of the day after that and the day after *that,* and wondered what she could do. But she was too polite to mention it now that he had been so generous with the candy.

Her indecision must have showed in her eyes, because he said, "Tomorrow, Sister, tomorrow . . . this is an important problem, and I must think until tomorrow. Ask me tomorrow about the next day."

Don Scarpo's "show and tell" was a great success. The next afternoon, when the Children were down for their naps, Sister got the list from Sister Cook and went across to Don Scarpo's.

"Listen, I was thinking, Sister," he said. "You do take them for a walk each day after siesta, don't you? Well, take them a different place each day. Then let each one draw a picture of what impressed him most, and tell the class about it."

Sister wasn't so sure that that was as perfect a solution as the candy had been, but she had respect enough for Don Scarpo to give it a try.

That afternoon she took the Children for a walk along the docks. Some Sister before her had taught them to walk in step, quick-step, and to recite as they walked:

> *Triqui-trín!*
> *Triqui-trán!*
> *Los maderos de San Juan,*
> *Piden queso, piden pan:*
> *Los de Roque, alfandoque,*
> *Los de Rique, alfeñique,*
> *Triqui-triqui-triqui-trán!*

It was a cheerful, gay little verse, and the militant tempo made them walk briskly, and saying the words gave each a chance to shout or murmur, whichever he felt like.

The other Children didn't reach out to Perico as they did to each other: they were beautiful, with the beauty of childhood; Perico, Sister had to admit to herself, was the homeliest child she had ever seen. Oh, he had two eyes, a nose, a mouth, a couple of ears, but he looked as though, when the clay of his face had been formed, the artist had petulantly smeared it up with his thumb: his nose was slightly askew, one eye was higher than the other, his teeth looked like a broken picket fence. So her heart went out to Perico; she reached for him more than for the others, whose beauty reflected God's goodness. Perico must have reflected that goodness too, but it was certainly not apparent at first. He was surly, morose, even disobedient. Not *bad:* who, at the age of five, can be *bad?* But he wasn't *good,* either. He just didn't have the easy disposition of most Children of five who are well fed, well scolded and well loved.

Well, but back to "show and tell": she took them walking along the docks: Joselito and Go (which was short for Guido, which was short for Guillermo); Rosario and María del Pilar; Mariucha and Tito, Perico and Sister.

They quick-stepped along the noisy, thronged dock street; the Children all wore red-and-white-striped tops and blue bottoms so one could hardly tell the girls from the boys, except for the girls' long braids and that they wore blue skirts instead of shorts. Sister Bertrille would have cut the girls' hair short (so much easier to look neat!), and let them

wear shorts too—but Sister Plácido had definite ideas
on that: girls wear long hair, boys, short; girls wear
skirts, boys, trousers. And that was that.

Sister Bertrille had an extra twenty minutes a day
of brushing and braiding; and the good Lord only
knew how much more time was spent in admonishing
the girls to Sit Like Ladies. Because if you're going
to wear skirts, you've *had* it: you've got to Sit Like a
Lady or else, even if you are only five years old.

Along the docks they went: the street was jammed
with trucks and handcarts and *públicos*—touring-car
taxis—and in this section of the city men seemed to
be louder, stronger, more cheerful. There weren't
many women. And there, in the water, the huge ships
towered, like black boat-shaped buildings, they were
that huge. Big, foot-high letters named each ship:
*CATHERINE LYKES; JEAN BULL; MAGAL-
LANES; SERENA; MORMACQUEEN* and *MIMITO
MARU.*

The *Magallanes* was a Spanish ship, Sister told
them; and Magallanes, who was called Magellan in
English, was the first man to sail round the world;
the *Mimito Maru* was Japanese, and *maru* meant
"steamship." She didn't know what *mimito* meant.

The Children were so impressed with the size of
the ships that Sister had little hope for "show and
tell" the next day. It was bound to be nothing but
black-hulled ships on blue water (though the harbor
water was actually green, children always paint water
blue). But the next day they surprised her.

Joselito drew a stevedore, big-shouldered and strong; Go drew a stalk of green bananas—he had seen them stacked in a pier shed, waiting to be loaded; Rosario drew a flag because he was good at drawing flags—he could make them seem to flap in the wind; María del Pilar drew a ship, but not like any of the ships they had seen, for this one had big sails on it, with pictures on the sails; Mariucha drew a woman with red lips and golden earrings and a bright red dress (where had she seen *her*?); and Tito, bless him, drew a black-hulled cargo ship, or Sister would have lost all faith in her knowledge of child psychology.

When Tito sat down she called on Perico. He shook his head. He hadn't finished.

She said, "That's all right, Perico. Show us what you have done, and tell us about the rest."

And then she was sorry. For the other Children went off into gales of laughter at sight of his drawing: he had drawn nothing but a piece of rope!

Sister quieted the Children with a *look*. "Tell us about it, Perico," she coaxed. But she didn't really dare to hope that he had anything to tell. He had spent the whole period drawing nothing but a rope.

He stood at ease before the class with one finger pointing, and said, "See? Look. If you look close, you can see: a rope isn't brown at all. It's brown and gray and green and blue and black and tan and silver and white; and a rope isn't just a rope, but it's a million tiny little threads wound around and around and around . . ."

The Children were staring, fascinated. So was Sister. It had never occurred to her that there was so much to a simple rope.

". . . and," Perico finished, "where they cut it off at the end, they tie it into a knot, and it whirls and sprays out like a brush, and, it's YELLOW!"

The Children fell back with astonishment.

Sister, gathering them together for wash-up before lunch, thought about Don Scarpo and how wise he was. Tomorrow, she would take them back to the beach, let them find the smallest things possible to discover the world of littleness. Don Scarpo's grocery store would be a fascinating place for them. And the fortress, with its sloping ramps and tunnels, even the cobbles on the streets and the designs on the wrought-iron balconies. There were *worlds* for them to discover!

# *Four*

It was all very easy to take Children for walks, and shop and do laundry and all that sort of pleasant everyday thing. But Sister Bertrille found that it wasn't very easy not to think about flying. Suddenly she had become obsessed with the idea of flight: everything reminded her of it. She watched the pigeons in the patio, how they ran, sweeping the air with their wings, and took off, and, at the airborne moment, tucked their landing gear up in under them. And every day the pelicans went by outside the windows, gliding in long, single-file lines; she took to counting them: one day a hundred and twenty-five went north, and seventy-three went south.

And then, one night, she had that dream—a dream more vivid than any she had had before. She dreamed that she got up, dressed, and went out onto the third-floor balcony outside the room she shared with Sister Narciso, Sister Cook, and Sister Laundress. White curtains divided the room into four neat alcoves where each nun had a stand, a bed, a chair, a small throw rug. The rugs seemed a shame, Sister

Bertrille thought, because the floor tiles were beautiful Moorish tiles, brought from Spain four hundred years before, and the colors in them were the loveliest blues and reds, and creamy white.

Out on the balcony, the moon blazed away, a hot-white tropical moon that sent a shattered path of light along the sea . . . and across that path of light went a soaring line of pelicans. Sister was gratefully certain that she was dreaming then, because she was quite sure that pelicans don't fly at night. But that was the only thing that convinced her, because everything else was so *real:* the wind whipped at her so hard that she had to cling to the damp, salt-sticky rail of the balcony.

And along came the pelicans, fourteen of them, black against the navy-blue sky, soaring in such unbelievably beautiful grace . . . Sister got up onto the railing, lifted her head, spread her arms, and took off after the last one.

Oh, it was glorious! No wondering where or how to fly, she simply followed the lead of the pelican in front of her, and he followed the one in front of him, and they soared and dipped, and the wind, instead of buffeting Sister, bore her up, as though this were a much more natural element for her than the earth where she habitually walked.

The pelican in front of her dipped, and with a horrible-delightful sensation, she dipped too, down close to the flagstaff on top of Fortress San Cristóbal.

For one dreadful moment she thought they were

going to light on the cross trees, and how would *that* look to the flagman in the morning, a Sister perched on the cross trees?

But the lead pelican angled his wings upward, and his head lifted, and up he went, soaring, until the fortress looked like a hacked-at square of white cheese in the moonlight—and after him went the thirteen other pelicans, and Sister, head tilted upward, nose pointed at the sky, arms angled so that her sleeves served as glider wings.

Suddenly the lead pelican sounded off, a short, sharp cry, and, like soldiers answering roll call, the others called something that sounded like "Haaahn!" When the fourteenth one had called out, Sister, without thinking, but being an obedient person, opened her mouth and called in a high, sweet voice, "Here!"

The pelican in front of her almost fell out of the air, which caused such turbulence that Sister got bounced about before he swept his great wings in long, strong strokes to get back into line again, and that put him quite a bit ahead of her, and she knew her arms weren't going to serve as well as his wings did, so she just glided on the air current, that fortunately, right there where the cold sea bordered the warm land, rushed upward in a towering wall that held her up, since there was some wind that moved the wall along.

Pelicans, when they fly, pull their long necks in and tuck their heads down between their shoulders, to lessen resistance to the air and make them fly better.

But now the pelican in front of Sister cautiously stretched his neck and turned around, got one quick look at her and said in a strangled voice, "Aaaagh!"

A strong rising updraft lifted Sister and pushed her practically into his tail feathers, and he thrashed his wings to get away from her, and the thrust of air thus created lifted her back into line.

The fourteenth pelican screeched, and the lead pelican swung out in a wide circle, turning back in on his own line so that he went into a power dive right below Sister, craning his neck and turning one gleaming eye up to look at her as he went under, the others following; and pretty soon they had straightened out into a line again, heading back the way they had come, Sister following through, all around the three-hundred-sixty-degree turn, then another hundred-eighty-degree half circle, and then they were all in straight file again, returning to the Convent of San Tanco.

Sister couldn't believe her eyes: instead of following the line of the sea and that rising wall of warm air that held them up so buoyantly, the pelicans headed straight for the convent—not the balcony, but the roof. The lead pelican dived straight under the clothesline and then rose on the other side to clear the roof wall, and the others followed after him, one, two, three, four, even to the fourteenth: Sister came in in a fast glide, grabbed the clothesline, and hung on, being blown from the back feet first, so

that she could see the pelicans soar up into the wind, make a right-angle turn, and head out toward that wall of air by the sea.

Her arms ached; her shoulders had almost been jerked out of their sockets. She worked her way, flapping in the wind, to the wall where the clothesline was attached: the wall blocked the wind, and she dropped gratefully to the floor of the roof and sat there, rubbing her shoulders, then put both arms around a heavy stone flowerpot and inched herself and the flowerpot to the top of the stairs that led down to the convent floor of the building.

It wasn't until she was back in bed, white curtains of her alcove fluttering in the wind, that it occurred to her to wonder how the lead pelican had known where to drop her off.

Then she chuckled to herself, for it had been only a dream after all; so she blessed herself and thanked God for such a lovely, exciting dream, and for the happy escape from it, and then began to bless her parents and her sisters and her brothers (all eight of them) and her godparents and Sister Plácido . . . She fell asleep again before she got to Don Scarpo and the sailors on the ship.

Everyone in a convent goes to chapel every morning with her eyes cast down (some say still closed in sleep, for it's five A.M.) and so it wasn't until Sister sat at the breakfast table that Sister Sixto glanced up at her, then away.

Sister Cook looked at Sister Bertrille, then down at her plate, then at something past Sister Bertrille's shoulder. Sister Plácido, at the head of the table, did not even look up. Sister Cook rose, gathered her dishes, cast Sister Bertrille what seemed to be a supplicating look, and ran to the kitchen.

Sister Laundress stood behind her chair, said her grace, and left, her eyes still closed.

Sister Sixto stared, turned beet-red, went to say something, glanced at Sister Plácido, and changed her mind.

Sister Sixto was looking at Sister Bertrille with what could only be called Dawning Realization. She put her hand over her mouth, said her grace in a rapid mutter, didn't look again at Sister Bertrille, but rushed out of there as though all her Old People were screaming at once, though the truth was, it was only just time for the Old Ones to begin waking up.

"You may be excused, Sisters," Sister Plácido murmured, and the other Sisters and Sister Bertrille got up, said their grace and left for their various tasks: to tend to the bookkeeping (the librarian had to double in brass and be bookkeeper too, only bookkeeper didn't mean to keep books, it meant, write down how much money came in, how much money went out each day, and Make it Balance).

So it wasn't until she went to wake up her Children that Sister Bertrille found out what it was that had made everyone look at her so peculiarly this morning.

She bent over Perico's bed to wake him up, and he opened his eyes and frowned at her; then suddenly his eyes brightened and he began to laugh, and he laughed and laughed, lying flat on his back in bed, staring up at Sister.

She couldn't help laughing with him, he looked so happy, lying there so cozy in his little bed and chuckling like a homely little old man who thought the world was funny.

Finally she said, "What is it, Perico? What's so wonderfully funny this morning?"

He looked at her slyly, his dark eyes sharing a secret with her.

"Does Sor Plácido let you wear a feather in your hat now?"

Sister's hand flew to her head, and there, in the fold of her cornette, was one large brown-and-gray quill feather.

A cold, frightened feeling crept from the toes of her black leather shoes to the top of her white cornette.

*The wind did it!* she assured herself, holding the feather in her hands.

A small, nasty voice inside her whispered, Oh, yeah? I'll just bet it did! The wind at about a thousand feet up over San Cristóbal, behind a line of pelicans!

"Nonsense!" Sister said in American to the voice, which always spoke to her in that language.

"What?" said Perico in Spanish. He didn't know any other language.

Sister smiled down at him. She'd put an end to this nonsense, once and for all. No souvenirs. She handed him the feather. "Here, Perico. This is for you."

His eyes sparkled. He took the feather gently, tenderly, held it close to his eyes. "Look, Sister: it's made up out of a million tiny feathers. See? Each little curlicue that comes up out of the spine is another feather, *complete*—with little curlicues coming out of *it!* The feather is made of feathers on feathers, and I'll bet, if I could see that good, even the feathers' feathers would have feathers!"

I'll get him a magnifying glass! she thought, and then, overwhelmed with ideas: Why not a microscope? And then, held down by practical considerations: we might *borrow* a microscope somewhere.

When the Children went down for their naps that afternoon—why do I use that phrase, "went down," she thought—then: Well, I take them upstairs, but their poor little bodies are so tired they plunge *down* into their little beds and are alseep before I can close the jalousies and turn on the fans.

Anyway, when they were down, she went to the library.

She found the *Encyclopedia Americana* and began with FEATHERS, which led her to PTERYLOGRAPHY, BIRD, AND FLIGHT; and she was reading FLIGHT when Sister Librarian came over to her and, glancing over her shoulder, said, "Oh, are you interested in FLINCH?"

"No," Sister Bertrille said, "Perico said that feathers have feathers on their feathers, and I was looking it up—" Then she stopped, because she realized that FEATHERS was not what she was reading.

That nasty voice inside her said in American, Oh, so you're looking something up for *Perico,* are you?

"Well," she said, "you know how an encyclopedia is: one thing leads to another—"

Sister Librarian was quiet. Very quiet. *Too* quiet. Then she said, "Sister, I ought to caution you—sometimes the Devil quotes Scripture to suit his purposes."

"Yes," said Sister Bertrille abstractedly, thinking that it wouldn't be unfair for her to look up PELICAN, since it was a pelican feather she had given Perico, and BIRDS had mentioned how feathers differed. Or *was* it a pelican feather, after all, if the wind had blown it there? . . . She got up, not noticing Sister Librarian, who tossed her head and stomped off, and got the ORLEY TO PHOTOGRAPHY volume, and looked up PELICAN.

They were four to six feet long, it said. She believed that. She herself was only four foot ten, and those birds had really dwarfed her. It said that their wingspan was six to nine feet—really, they were monsters; no wonder they could fly!

At last she found something for Perico: the feathers were brown, spotted with silvery-gray. Yes, assuredly, it *was* a pelican feather she had given to him.

That cold, frightened feeling crept over her again.

Sister Librarian said to her, "Three o'clock."

"Oh," Sister Bertrille jumped up, put the books back, and rushed out to get her Children up and washed and dressed for their walk. She would take them to the beach.

The next days were days of scalding, bleaching
sunlight, and steady salt breeze; of tasks, ordinary
and extraordinary tasks, for Sister Plácido sent her
on odd errands while the Children slept: once to a
lawyer (Sister Sixto always went with her, for the
Sisters were not allowed to go alone; but Sister
Bertrille was the actual emissary); once to the Mu-
nicipal Health Department for consultation with a
dietician; once to Padín's to discuss prices of cloth;
once to the dentist to discuss orthodontia for Perico;
once to the wholesale food dealer (they went to Don
Scarpo only for the daily things that might spoil in
a subtropical country).

Other days Sister Plácido would call her into the
office and just *talk*—about *all* her problems: how to
keep Sister Cook and Sister Laundress from squab-
bling; that it was best to have Sister Librarian, when
she showed signs of nervousness, to do some purely
mechanical tasks; that an occasional dash of rum was
in order for the Old Ones at fiesta time. Sister Bertrille thought no more of this than that Sister Plácido
needed someone to talk to. If she had *thought*, she
might have realized that a Superior seldom chooses
one of her subordinates for a confidante. But she
*didn't* think. She only sympathized with Sister Plácido for all her problems, made an occasional sug-
gestion, but never once guessed that Sister might
have plans for her.

One day at lunch, for spiritual reading, Sister Plácido read to them from the life of Saint Joseph
Cupertino, who had embarrassed all his superiors by

floating about in the air. This was to give the Sisters a subject for meditation for the rest of the day.

After lunch Sister Sixto caught Sister Bertrille on the second-floor balcony.

"I wanted to speak with you a moment, Sister." Sister Sixto, humble enough at any time, seemed to be crawling.

"Yes, Sister?"

"Sister, many very holy people don't realize that they are holy, because they're so humble, and so all kinds of strange things happen to them . . ."

Sister Bertrille was late for her Children. If they slept too long in the afternoon they would not fall asleep at night. She wished Sister Sixto would get to the point.

"Yes, Sister?" She leaned toward the Children's dormitory.

"Many holy people are very anxious that people not know that they are so holy, so they try to hide it, but God lets the poor others know"—Sister Sixto folded her big hands and raised her eyes to heaven— "by granting *Favors*."

"*Favors?*"

"Like bilocation," Sister Sixto murmured humbly. "Like levitation."

"Oh. Yes, yes, of course!" Sister Bertrille felt bad. She hadn't meditated on the Subject for the Day at all. And here she was, trying to brush poor Sister Sixto off, when she had just wanted to discuss what she had been thinking about all day. What was the subject? Oh! Sure! Bilocation, levitation—Saint Joseph Cupertino!

Sister Bertrille pulled herself together, to try to give Sister Sixto some measure of warmth and understanding and at the same time to get to her Children to get them up.

"Listen, Sister," she said, "I'm sure that it really was a favor to Saint Joseph—the flying, I mean. Oh, it embarrassed him and everybody else, but at the same time the actual flight, the feeling of flying—must have been simply wonderful!"

She squeezed Sister Sixto's hand, tried to show her in a look all the affection she felt for her, and ran.

She halted the Children outside Don Scarpo's, and he came to the doorway, and she asked him where he thought they should go that day.

"Oh!" He smoothed his big mustache and said, "Oh, my Sister, the place for you to go is to my cousin's ship chandlery; it's at the marina and he has all the fascinating equipment to go in ships, and at the same time there is a big brown tame pelican—you'll love to talk to it!"

Sister was nodding enthusiastically, right up to the point where Don Scarpo suggested that she have a chat with the pelican. Then, as Perico showed Don Scarpo his pelican feather, Sister began to have a cold feeling in the heels of her black leather shoes.

# Five

It was a lovely walk that day; Perico felt important and consequently he was pleasant and agreeable. Sister and the Children easily found their way to Don Scarpo's cousin's ship chandlery. There they examined with delight all the things he showed them from the rivets that hold great ships together to an anchor as big as a door; lanterns that swung in things called gimbals and cleats and chocks and deck boards and duckboards and compasses and sextants and clamps and buckets and mops and brass polish. So many of the things that go on ships were made of shiny yellow-gold brass. Don Scarpo's cousin said that maybe that was so because sailors had to be kept busy on long voyages, and polishing the brass gave them something to do.

Then he took them out onto the sun-grayed plank dock. He fished a bucketful of minnows from a bait well and took Sister and the Children up to a handsome-ugly gray and brown pelican who squatted in somber solitude on a thick creosote-black piling.

"Good afternoon, Don Pipo," Don Scarpo's cousin said to the pelican, very respectfully.

The pelican turned his head slowly, looked at the Children, looked at Sister, then opened his mouth—wide—at Don Scarpo's cousin, who tossed a dipperful of little fish into it, water and all.

Sister was astonished! The big pouch under the pelican's bill was like a net: the fish stayed inside, while all the water sieved out and ran down his breast and onto the piling. Well, she thought to God, *that's* a pretty nice arrangement, otherwise he'd drown in all that sea water that he scoops up with his fish. She had seen them dive from as high as twenty feet in the air, land with a great splash, and come up flapping and dripping with a mouthful of fish.

Everyone hated to go when it was time, they had had such a good time watching Don Pipo the pelican eat his little snack and clack his big bill in appreciation after each dipperful had been strained and swallowed.

Sister was a little relieved when the visit was over, though, because Don Scarpo's remark about having a chat with the pelican had unnerved her a bit, even though she couldn't admit it, even to herself. Things had been all slightly awry lately, what with people talking at cross-angles and dreams about flying—she wouldn't have been much surprised at all if the pelican, Don Pipo, *had* had something to say.

So it was with a sigh of relief that she thanked Don Scarpo's cousin enthusiastically, prodded the Children

into expressing their thanks—and then, as she turned to leave, *the pelican winked at her!*

She shut her eyes and looked away, afraid to see if anyone had noticed that wink. She tucked her hands in her sleeves, cast down her eyes, lined up her charges, took Perico's hand, and started them off.

*"Triqui-trín! Triqui-trán! . . ."*

Pelicans don't wink, she kept telling herself all the way home. Particularly not at *people*. He had just had something in his eye, that was all. Yeah, said the nasty voice in American, he had something in his eye, all right: a conspiratorial gleam!

"Nonsense!" Sister said aloud.

Beside her Perico said, "What's *nonsense?*"

She told him in Spanish, and he laughed and said, "Oh. You say that a lot, you know."

"I know," she admitted. "I'll try to stop."

"No." Perico's little-old-man face wrinkled up in thought. "Don't stop. It's nice to know you go around thinking about nonsense all the time."

Sister blushed. It *was* nonsense for a full-grown Sister to be running around with her head full of thoughts about flying, instead of holy things and her Children and the other work to be done around the convent. She would stop it this instant. She joined in the chanting of the Children and managed not to think about flying except fleetingly until later that night, when the lights were out and she was in bed.

The moon was just less than full, and the wind was strong tonight. She heard a flight of pelicans go

by, heard their odd roll call: "*Haaahn. . . . Haaahn.
. . .*" Unconsciously she counted the cries, until she
came to fourteen; then there were no more—that was
*her* flight!

She sighed, wondering if they missed her little
piping "*Heeere!*" tonight. She said a prayer, then
another distracted one, and then she heard them
again: they had circled the convent, and the leader
again sounded his roll-call cry: "*Haaahn!*"

And then came the others, thirteen of them, their
cries calling to and tempting her, inviting her out into
the glorious night sky with them.

Before she knew what she was doing she was up
and dressed and standing on the balcony railing, her
full skirts blowing about, clinging to the roof cornice
over her head, waiting to see if they came again.

And they did. They came. She heard the steady
thrumming of their wings as they beat up-wind over
the roof, then turned and sailed in a beautiful, long,
soaring, dipping gliding line—straight for the balcony
where she stood.

The leader dived in close to her, sounded his long
cry, and turned in a steep banking turn and swept
away toward the sea; the others, each one calling to
her in turn, followed in his wake.

Sister took a deep breath, pushed away from the
wall, threw up her head and spread her arms and
soared out after the last pelican in line toward the
city wall, the edge of the sea, and that rising, *lifting*
wall of air.

The flying was glorious tonight, terrifying and exciting and thrilling beyond anything that could hap-

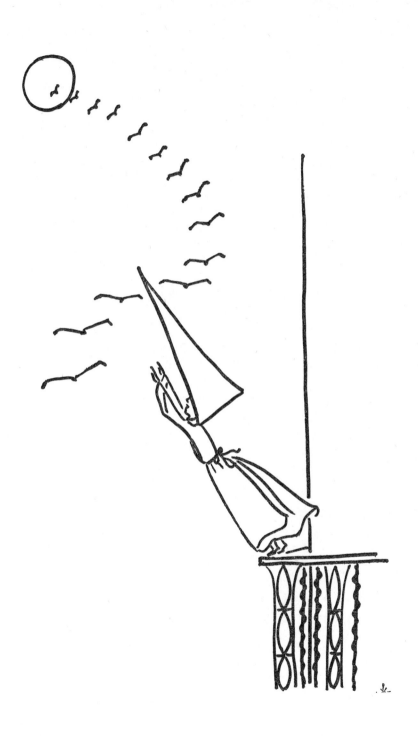

pen to one in dreams, because it was real and she knew it.

And the pelicans knew her now, and accepted her. They even had come after her, if circling the convent were any indication. And after all why shouldn't the leader have known where to bring her home that first night? Really, a pelican could be as observant as anyone else, and it would certainly be easy enough for him to have seen where the women who wore blue dresses and big white bonnets lived.

The stars were so thick that Sister Bertrille felt as though she were flying among them, and the soft whirr of the pelicans' flight and their long cries on the wind lifted her heart to God, to praise Him for this thing He had made possible: flight.

And then, thinking of God, she remembered that obedience was one vow she had made, and she should be home in bed right now. But then, Sister Plácido hadn't *said,* "Go to bed." Sister just took it for granted that she *was* in bed.

She thought about the Holy Founder of her Order, and what wisdom had been his, and wondered why he hadn't made the promises more specific, since he knew he was dealing with the minds of women. Poverty, chastity, obedience—were pretty broad terms . . .

It could hardly be a sin to fly—to do anything like this, that was so beautifully *natural* and *good*. She danced with the Children: schottische and polka and Mexican hat; she had played baseball and basketball with the girls at Saint Scholastica's back in Washington. So what was the matter with flying?

What impressed her most—impressed and exhila-

rated—was the *quality* of the air up here: so cool and
sweet and clear, like cold water from a mountain
spring. It had no smell whatsoever, only cleanness—
not the cleanness of soap or paint or polish, but the
cleanness of nothingness, of purity—of perfection. And
*so* clear! She could see all the lights of the city, the
shimmering sea in the moonlight, phosphorescent
streaks where fish swam; across the smooth glaze of
the harbor water were the lights of Cataño, and
beyond that the shadows of the hills, and in the core
of the hills a few lights that were the army camp.

Clear and sweet and pure was that air, and heady—
it was what people *should* be breathing instead of all
that smoke and grime and dust and smell on earth.

They went farther than ever along the coast that
night, past Escambrón, toward Condado—and then
the wind shifted, the lead pelican swung slowly
around in a broad half circle, and they headed back
for San Juan. Just before they came to Fortress San
Cristóbal, which was just before Convento San Tanco,
the leader sounded off his cry and the others answered in the high, thin air, their full, deep an-
swers—and Sister, in the spirit of gay, insouciant
comradeship, sang out, "*Heeeere!*"

The pelican in front of her never wavered. He
knew she was there tonight.

The leader began the long, crosswind descent, crab-
bing into the wind but setting his true course for the
convent. Sister copied the angle of their bodies and
wings, and as the leader swooped in under the clothesline she reached up, it slapped her wrists, she closed
her fingers over it.

Thin arms wrapped around her legs and pulled her down to earth.

Sister Plácido had been standing on the roof, waiting for her.

Sister Bertrille staggered a little in the buffeting wind as Sister Plácido set her on her feet, and the older nun had to hold her down while they crossed the roof to the stairs.

It wasn't until they stood outside the door of Sister's room that Sister Plácido spoke. "Go to bed," she said. "And stay there until the rising bell. I shall speak to you later about this."

Poor Sister Bertrille tossed and turned all night. If Sister had just scolded her then and there, she could have brought forth all her arguments about there being nothing really wrong with flying, and she wasn't even causing scandal by flying around with the pelicans, because it was night, and no one saw her . . . But *this* way she could only lie there in an anguish of guilty feelings and uneasiness. What *was* the standard penance for flying?

In the morning, at breakfast, Sister Plácido said to Sister Laundress, "You will take the kindergarten this morning, Sister"; and to Sister Bertrille: "I will see you in my office immediately after breakfast."

Sister Plácido's office was as cool, aloof, and reserved as Sister herself. She had Sister Bertrille sit down; then she tipped her fingers together like a church steeple and contemplated them for a long time, while Sister Bertrille squirmed and tried not to appear to squirm.

Then: "Were you aware of your actions last night?"

Sister Bertrille lowered her eyes. "Yes, Sister."

"Ah." Another long silence, during which Sister Bertrille tried to guess what the next question might be, but she couldn't. There was nothing inside her head but a hot, burning, miserable hollow.

"When," Sister Plácido asked, "did you discover that you had this—ability?"

"The day I got here, Sister."

Sister's eyebrows asked the next question, so Sister Bertrille explained how she had thought she was dreaming the first time she had followed the pelicans, but that then she had known it was real, because she'd been reading about aerodynamics, and it *was* just barely possible . . . She recited the formula: "If *lift* plus *thrust* is greater than *load* plus *drag*, the result is flight."

"Ah. Then you don't feel that this is something from God?"

"Oh, good grief, *no*, Sister! Except only in that He made the laws that govern these things. For example, the formula for swimming is *water* plus *paddle your hands and kick your feet*, and you *swim*. Air is an element too, like water, and if you follow the right formula, you fly."

"A-*ha*. Then may I take it that since you know the magic formula in order to fly, you also know how to *reverse* this formula in order *not* to fly?"

"Oh, yes, Sister. You see, it would be just, *load* plus *drag* exceeding *lift* plus *thrust*. It's not magic at all, no more than that stones are hard, and fire burns, and water flows downhill—"

Sister Plácido held up her hand. "Then we must

endow you with more load and drag. *But!* I should not encourage you to eat more in order to weigh more, for that could lead to the sin of gluttony, instead of the mere foolishness in which you are now enmeshed. Also, you cannot practically walk about clinging to heavy objects."

"No, Sister."

"Nor would it be seemly, though it *might* be practical, for you to pull an anchor along after you."

Was Sister Plácido smiling? No, it was just a trick of light, that faint glimmer in her eyes that reminded Sister Bertrille of the pelican who had winked.

Sister Plácido stood up, indicating that the interview was over. "We shall think on this further."

"Yes, Sister."

"In the meanwhile—*no* means of locomotion except those afforded to the rest of us. Is that clear?"

"Yes, Sister."

"One other thing: Sister Sixto has conceived the notion that you've been flying about because of your great holiness."

"Oh, *no!*"

"Oh, yes. You will make it a point to disillusion Sister Sixto, before she tries to canonize you. *But!*"

Sister Bertrille jumped. Those *buts!* of Sister's were like pistol shots.

"*But!* You will *not* achieve this by acting *un*holy, do you understand? Simply explain to her the principles of aerodynamics as you have explained them to me, without, of course, referring to any actual experiences."

"Yes, Sister." Sister Bertrille went out onto the gallery, and there was Sister Sixto, coming from the kitchen. They met in the middle of the wide patio.

"Uh—Sister?"

Sister Sixto stopped as though she had been hoping Sister Bertrille might condescend to speak to her, a mere normal human being, strong of flesh and weak of spirit.

Sister Bertrille came right to the point and asked Sister Sixto, "Have you ever studied aerodynamics?"

Sister Sixto gulped and shook her head.

Sister Bertrille was angry with herself for having asked such a stupid question of Sister Sixto, who would have studied geriatrics, not aerodynamics.

Sister Sixto said, "Sister Bertrille, I have been wanting to ask you a great favor: would you please pray for my poor uncle in Spain? He has been ill for so long. His name is Rosario Sánchez—Sánchez de Luna—" Sister Sixto was talking in a rush, the way one does when one feels he has no right to impose.

Sister Bertrille, touched, said, "Of course. We'll all pray for your uncle. But what I wanted to talk to you about was that day on the roof, when you saved me by jumping on me—"

"Oh, Sister, I've been wanting to apologize to you about that! If I'd *known* I'd have *never*—"

Known. Known what? Well, never mind. "Sister, that was a perfectly natural thing, I want you to understand that. When you think that though I weigh only seventy-five pounds my cornette is the same size as yours—"

"And I weigh a hundred eighty," Sister Sixto said humbly.

"Perfectly proper for your height," Sister Bertrille assured her, and plowed on: "What I was getting to is that, if something is light enough, and moves fast enough, and has wings, it will fly. And my cornette is almost like wings. And that's what happened to me there on the roof that day. And that's *all.* Do you understand?"

"Oh, yes, Sister."

The lunch bell rang at that moment, and they had to collect their charges. Sister Bertrille was silently congratulating herself that she had convinced Sister Sixto of her unholiness without actually doing something awful. She was just pleasurably remembering her perfectly lucid exposition when Sister Sixto said pleadingly:

"You will pray for my uncle, won't you?" And she made to Sister Bertrille a little obeisance that was a cross between a curtsy and a genuflection.

Sister Bertrille went about her duties with a yearning heart. No means of locomotion *except* meant just that: no flying. She didn't blame Sister Plácido really, but if Sister only knew what it was like up there . . .

She began to listen for the pelicans and watch for them, and was liable to stop in mid-sentence and stand openmouthed when a flight went overhead.

She envied a fat-bellied C-119 cargo plane that roared over the city every other day.

She gazed sadly on the pigeons that picked at crumbs and strutted about the patio of the convent, thinking that if she were they, she certainly wouldn't be plunking about on the cobblestones; she would be soaring like a leaf, high in the blue.

And that was her downfall. If only she had been able to turn the back of her mind to all flying things . . . but even the fat cockroaches that flew circling the electric light at night reminded her of the glories of flight.

She thought about flying, she dreamed about flying, and one night, when she had tossed and turned and at last fallen into an exhausted half sleep, the flight of fourteen pelicans circled the convent.

The wind was high that night, but she could hear the thrust of their great powerful wings as they went on the up-wind pull past the balcony, then heard the leader give his roll-call cry, and each answering call came closer and closer, so she knew that they were circling again.

She was half asleep. She really didn't know what she was doing. Far back in her sleep-heavy mind she heard a voice like Sister Plácido's—and at that moment the fourteenth pelican skimmed by, crying right into the open window, and drowned out the voice.

The cold air above the convent wakened Sister thoroughly, but before she came to the full realization of the seriousness of her offense they were far

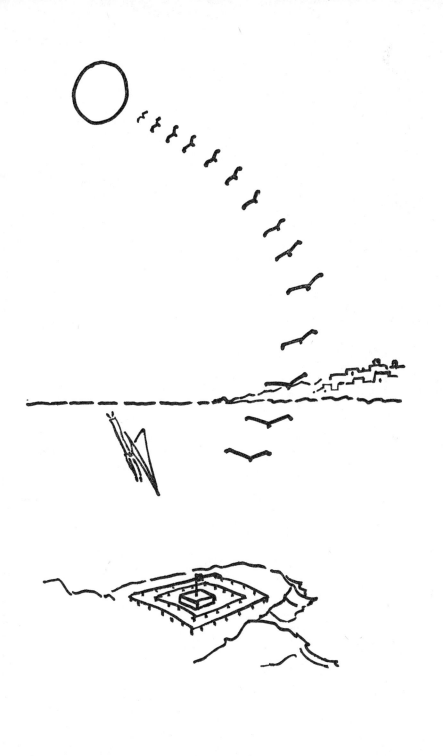

out over the sea. She had to depend on the pelicans. She never could have flown without them, for they, with their big bodies and wide wings, found the paths through the air that would hold up a body as heavy as hers. So she had to follow along in the wake of the last pelican, willy-nilly, praying that they would take her back to San Tanco, and seeing at the same time that he was swinging in a great wide circle that would pass them over the Castle of El Morro at least a mile away from the convent.

The strong offshore wind bore them up and up, higher and higher, until the harbor was a small bowl of black water below them, its edges trimmed in gold lights. Then they had passed over the harbor and were descending rapidly toward the mountains that rose behind Cataño. They shot downward in a swift, steep, dizzy glide, aiming directly at a blaze of light that came up at them like the headlight of an onrushing locomotive. The air was rougher as they closed in on that mountainside, and the square of light turned out to be one of those fenced-off places that the army has here and there, with strictly secret stuff inside them. At a hundred feet they zeroed in on the floodlighted, square white windowless building, passing over a wire-mesh fence topped with barbed wire; an open space, flood-lighted; another fence; another open space where vicious-looking dogs prowled; more barbed wire—and an armed guard pacing before the only opening in the building, a door.

# Six

Inside the building with no windows, Corporal Page, half asleep, scanned the radarscope.

"Here come those pelicans again," he said. He began to count them softly to himself: "One, two, three, four, five . . ."

His partner, Smitty, looked over his shoulder at the smooth line of blips coming onto the screen. He checked the weather report, said indifferently, "Offshore wind. They do that every time: come right in on the wind and then take off up over the mountain. It must be like sleigh riding for them."

As Page finished counting, Petrovsky, the third man, put down his cards and came to watch.

". . . thirteen, fourteen, fifteen—" Page said. Then: "There they go, up"—as the line of blips angled upward toward the right-hand corner of the screen. Then, as they watched, the last blip slipped out of line, slipped under the one in front of it, slipped back again, lower—

"Oops! Somebody shot one."

The last blip fluttered, like a falling leaf, and went down and off the screen.

"Fifty dollars' fine," Smitty said.

Petrovsky licked his lips. "If they catch him."

"It's too easy," Page said. "It's always some farmer fresh from the States, thinking he's getting a six-foot hawk. He'll bring it in to show off—they always do."

Smith, Petrovsky, and Page stood there a moment, staring at the empty screen. The air-conditioning machinery kicked on, and they stood there listening to it, thinking of sleigh riding, hawk shooting, ice skating, there in that bombproof, soundproof, light-proof little room.

# *Seven*

The line of pelicans zeroed in on the floodlighted building, and just before they hit, the lead pelican thrust his great body upward with long strokes of his wings, like a swimmer pulling for the surface. After him, one behind the other, each of the great birds made long, swooping thrusts, pulling himself up out of the down draft caused by the side of the mountain, reaching for the current of air at the top that would carry him out to sea again.

Sister Bertrille *felt* the air drop out from under her, saw the pelican in front of her drive his wings down like pistons. She wrenched herself out of her reverie, sideslipped, twisted, sideslipped again, feeling the bumps of air from the pelican's wings as she slid helplessly under him. They pulled away from her, up the side of the mountain and Sister Bertrille fell, like a falling leaf, and landed with a skidding thump inside the compound, raising quite a cloud of dust. When she had caught her breath she swung over and sat up, but painfully. She saw through the settling dust a pair of very shiny black field boots with dust sifting onto them and, above them, the shiny black muzzle of a carbine pointing at her.

She was careful not to move. Behind her, through the mesh of the fence, the dogs panted, snarled, tore at the fence to get at her.

The dust settled farther and she saw that the man holding the gun was the biggest man she had ever seen. Now Sister Bertrille was so small that most people looked to her twice as big as they actually were; but this man *was* big to begin with. Besides which, Sister was still sitting on the ground, so he looked three times as big. Her mouth fell open.

At the same time, the dust finished settling and the soldier got a look at her. His mouth dropped open.

Had they been dentists, they'd have had quite an opportunity to examine each other's fillings, but as it was, they simply stared, openmouthed, neither one able to grasp the simple reality of what was happening, which was that he was seeing a nun where no nun was supposed to be, and she was still stunned from her fall and seeing a giant right out of the fairy tales she read to the children, and hearing monsters scratching and snarling behind her.

He recovered first. He was a soldier, and a soldier is supposed to be able to adapt quickly to any situation. He remembered his General Orders. He gripped the carbine more firmly and said shakily, "Halt!" And then, in case this was a Puerto Rican nun: "*¡Alto!*"

"I *am* halted," she said in a small, frightened voice.

"I can see that," he said, "but that's what I'm *supposed* to say: 'Halt' three times, and then fire."

Sister shrank into herself.

"That is, I fire if you don't halt. But you're halted, okay, so it's okay. That is, *that much* is okay."

"Oh." She eased her position a little, and several twinges of pain stabbed her. She held still. "What happens next?"

"Then I say for you to identify yourself."

"Oh!" She brightened. "That's easy. I'm Sister Ber—" She stopped, horrified, thinking about how she was going to explain *this* to Sister Plácido. She hung her head and said to her lap, "I'm Sister Bertrille, of the Convent of San Tanco in San Juan. And I don't even know where I am."

"You're in a Security Area, that's where you are," the soldier said. "And what I'd like to know is how the heck you *got* in here."

Cautiously, keeping the carbine trained on her, he glanced about, but saw nothing amiss with the fences, the barbed wire, the dogs.

"I . . ." Sister's voice died out. He wouldn't believe her anyway. He'd think she was being fresh. And she didn't believe in letting people who were pointing guns at her think she was being fresh. So she said meekly, "What next, after I identify myself?"

"There's a few more steps," he said, "but I'm going to skip them, and yell for help." He threw out his chest and roared, "SERGEANT OF THE GUARD! POST FOUR!" He frowned helplessly at Sister and added, "ON THE DOUBLE!"

Another man came—the Sergeant of the Guard, no doubt—and stood staring down at Sister, biting his lip.

"You better get up," he said, and drew his gun, a large .45. There was an ominous click-click-*clack* as he cocked it, aimed it at her, and then self-consciously sort of *held* it.

"I feel like a fool," he said.

"What d'y'think *I* feel like?" the large soldier muttered.

Sister tried to get up, but all those twinges and a few more stabbed at her again. "Could you help me, please?"

Both men stepped back a pace, then looked sheepish, but held their ground. Any guard who knows judo knows better than to give his hand to someone. But then the sergeant passed his .45 to the soldier and said, "So shoot me too." He went around behind Sister and lifted her to her feet, then leaped out of range and retrieved his weapon.

Sister shook out her skirt, adjusted her cornette, tucked her hands in her sleeves. "What now?"

Apparently that had been in the sergeant's mind too, for he opened his mouth and bawled, "OFFICER IN CHARGE! POST FOUR!"

Several other voices echoed his cry, reminding Sister of the pelicans, and she wished violently that she were *with* the pelicans, instead of standing here embarrassing a lot of soldiers. She was embarrassed herself. Sooner or later, they were going to ask *that question* again; and what was she going to say?

Pretty soon along came a nice-looking young lieutenant, and the other two didn't say a thing: they just stood there and let him see for himself what they had caught.

He blinked. But he was such a nice young man, his good manners were a reflex, for he bowed, smiled, said, "Good evening, ma'am—" Then it struck him. She was there, in the middle of *his* Security Area—where no one *could* be: past fences and vicious dogs and two guards, there she was.

He bowed his head and struck his brow with his fist. "Oh, *no*."

"I'm so sorry," Sister said abjectly.

Those reflex good manners made him say, "Oh, that's all right—" He broke off. "No, it isn't! Ma'am —how did you get here?"

"I—oh, I don't know how to tell you—and you won't believe me when I do—" She was exhausted, frightened, bewildered. She looked at the three trying-to-be-kind but thunderstruck faces and burst into tears.

They were the three sickest-looking men that had ever worn the United States uniform.

She was aware of their misery, and stopped crying as soon as she could, and blew her nose and said, "What do we do now?" and smiled at them waterily, and that broke them up completely.

"Ma'am," said the lieutenant, "we'll have to—

well, you—" He said lamely, "You *could* be a Puerto Rican in disguise—they come that little."

The schoolteacher in her recited the lesson she had learned in the Mission Training School. "Puerto Ricans are Americans too," she said primly, though she didn't really believe it.

"Don't I know it," the sergeant groaned. "The minute they don't like what I'm saying they *no spik inglis.*"

"Maybe they forget how, when they're excited," Sister suggested.

The lieutenant cleared his throat. "Ma'am, excuse me, but this isn't getting us anywhere. I'm afraid we'll have to take you into custody."

Sister let out a little yelp of fright. She couldn't help it. *Custody*—that meant jail, didn't it? She caught up her rosary and began to pray—more fervently than she ever had before in her whole devout life.

"Hey!" said the sergeant. "None of that!"

The big soldier glared at him.

The lieutenant said coldly, "Why not?"

"Okay, okay, I'm sorry, go ahead, go ahead," the sergeant muttered.

But Sister had already dropped the rosary, tucked her hands into her sleeves, closed her eyes, and went right on praying—only not so overtly.

# *Eight*

Outside the three fences, in the Security Office, Sister sat in a heavy wooden armchair, her feet not quite touching the floor, praying silently. What for, she didn't know. She just prayed. In the doorway stood a man with a gun. Across the room sat another man with a gun.

At one desk, a corporal talked on the phone with Counter-Intelligence; at another, a sergeant was talking to the chief of the San Juan police.

A lieutenant, not the one with the reflex good manners, but one named Shannon, sat at the desk opposite Sister, writing things down. She tried to pay attention to his questions but couldn't help listening to the sergeant and the corporal and their conversations.

"Name?" asked Lieutenant Shannon. "Address? ... Age? ... Place of birth? ... Height? ... Weight?"

Sister answered him distractedly.

"Blue dress and big white bonnet," the sergeant

said into his phone. Then he called across to Lieutenant Shannon, "Convent of San Tanco! T-a-n-c-o."

"That checks," Shannon said, and smiled at Sister, a quick, small smile, but it was the first one she'd seen in a long time.

"I'm the kindergarten teacher," she confided, encouraged by even that small a smile.

"Yes s'st'r," he said patiently, and she thought with enormous, enveloping relief, A *Catholic* boy! Only a kid who had marched in line through parochial schools said, "Yes s'st'r," in that tone of voice. She pretended she hadn't found out his secret, but the surge of confidence sounded in her voice, she couldn't help *that*.

"I have seven darling little Children," she said. "All five years old: Joselito, Go, Rosario, María del Pilar, Mariucha, Tito, and Perico."

"Yes s'st'r," he said in deference to the habit she wore, "but—how do we know you're a real nun?"

That was a stunning thought! How did they know she was a real nun? If she could just prove to them she was really a Sister, then they might let her go, and if they only would, she would *crawl* back to San Juan and never even think about flying again! How could she prove she was a Sister?

"Sisters who travel carry orders, just like army people, only in Latin, you know, signed and sealed by their superiors . . ." Only she hadn't planned to travel, and no superior in her right mind would endorse the kind of travel or the destination she

had chosen that night. So she had no orders. Only
the habit she wore.

Lieutenant Shannon was waiting for her to pro-
duce a set of orders.

"I know all the Latin of the unchangeable parts
of the Mass . . ."

Lieutenant Shannon, if she knew boys who said
"yes s'st'r" in that tone of voice, was right at this
moment being torn apart emotionally: *if* she were a
real Sister, he'd cheerfully die for her; if she weren't,
he'd equally cheerfully shoot her dead.

The sergeant hung up his phone. "On the way,"
he announced.

The corporal hung up his phone. "Coming right
over."

Sister shuddered. If she could only convince *these*
men that she was a real Sister, before she had to get
involved with San Juan police, Counter-Intelligence
and things like that! She repeated her offer to say
the Latin.

Lieutenant Shannon shook his head. "See, Sister,"
he explained, "if the Russians wanted to send a spy
who looked like a nun, the first thing they'd make
darned sure she knew would be Latin. And prayers.
And the Mass. And that she'd babble about her
darling Children . . ."

Sister flushed.

"Well," he defended himself hotly, "wouldn't
they?"

She had to admit it. They would.

"Anyway," Shannon said, "*we* don't have the authority to turn you loose."

Something died a little in the very inside of Sister. Outside that, but still inside, she began praying again.

"Sister?"

There was faint echo of the parochial-school boy in Shannon's deep voice.

"Yes?"

"How *did* you get in there?" His eyes slid away. "And *why*?"

She took a deep breath. "If I told you just like that," she snapped her fingers, "you *couldn't* believe me. So I'll begin at the beginning, all right? I'll tell you the whole story . . ." Her voice dwindled.

Every man in the room was tense, strained, listening to what she would have to say.

And suddenly she realized that what was at stake here was not that one small Sister come out unshamed and unscathed from a rather harrowing experience, but something larger, more important. What mattered more was their *esprit de corps:* the pride these men had in themselves, in their Security Area, in the fact that no one, But No One, could get in there, through their fences, their dogs, their guns, their training, everything they had dedicated their lives to. The protection they gave to whatever was secret in that building was each one's individual contribution to the defense of his country, and *that* mattered more to them—and really, was more important than that she go unexposed, unridiculed, unpunished.

She looked at each one in turn: the sergeant, the corporal, the men with the guns, the lieutenant.

In magnificent obliteration of self, she announced, "I flew, behind some pelicans."

The silence seeded, grew, fanned out, overwhelmed them.

"*Oy*," said the sergeant. "A *nut*."

"Not from where I sit," Shannon said. To Sister he said coldly, "Where'd you stash the parachute?"

"Oh, not in a *plane*—" Sister violently wished she hadn't told them. "Just *me*. I'm light—and when the wind's right, I just ride the currents, the way the pelicans do."

"How does your superior feel about that?" Shannon asked. He'd been brought up on Saint Joseph Cupertino, too.

"Oh-h-h," she said, "not very happy. I didn't intend to tonight, it was—well—like sleepwalking."

"Most people who sleepwalk out a window go splash on the ground," the sergeant said.

"I did too, when I hit that downdraft," Sister said.

Shannon laughed. "How do you know about downdrafts?"

"I've been studying aerodynamics"—she felt the chill descend and enclose them—"because I wanted to find out why I kept being blown off the ground here when it never happened to me back home in the States!"

The chill congealed. She couldn't blame them. Why should a real nun study aerodynamics?

Each man busied himself at something. Sister's fingers found her rosary. As each bead slipped over the green silk cord, another prayer brought a measure of comfort. The clock ticked loudly. The sergeant lit up a pipe that smelled like smoke, apples, and chocolate. Shannon bent over his desk, doodling on a sheet of paper.

The corporal went to the window, peered out at the floodlighted field outside.

Sister finished her rosary, kissed the crucifix, clung to it. Her feet were going to sleep, because they didn't reach the floor. She slid forward on the chair, and the men with the guns tensed, moved their weapons gently.

"My feet are asleep," she explained. She tapped her feet against the chair legs, and the sensation was almost painful. She said, hesitantly, "How long . . . ?"

Gallantry is natural to men. The sergeant who had adjudged her a nut said, "Not long."

Sister smiled reassuringly at the men with the guns, slid forward on the chair, got her feet to the floor. She craned her neck, saw that Lieutenant Shannon wasn't doodling at all: he had drawn a pencil sketch of a lovely house with a sloping lawn, trees—and below that he had a floor plan.

"Oh, that's beautiful!"

He glanced up, made a light line bolder. "I wanted to be an architect, once."

Sister thought about that. Then: "Why didn't you?"

He erased a door through a wall. "Because you can't be two things. I wanted to be a soldier too. And you can't build houses and soldier, both, so the time came when I had to choose."

"And why did you choose . . . this?" She glanced about at the bare walls, the empty field visible through the window, the uncomfortable furnishings —even the uniforms they wore looked stiff and uncomfortable.

"Well—" He glanced at the other men, then said swiftly, "Look at the mess the world is in. *Somebody* has to do something about it, and I figure it's up to us."

Sister was electrified. "How about you?" she said to the sergeant.

"Me?" He rubbed his head. "I'm too old to think I can straighten the world out. I just like the life."

"And you?" she said to the man with the gun by the door.

He shook his head, staring at the wall.

"How about you?" she said to the corporal.

"Not me," he said. "All I want of this army is *out*. They caught me, and here I am, and I have left six months, four days, seven hours—and thirty minutes."

The other man with the gun grinned, so Sister said to him, "How about you?"

His face froze. He didn't look at her.

Shannon said gently, "It's a mistake for a guard to let a prisoner engage him in conversation."

"Oh." Sister sat back, feeling self-consciously like Mata Hari. The world was certainly in a mess. And if anyone could straighten it out, it would be men like these: the dedicated one, the one who "liked the life," and the one who hated the job but did it because it had to be done. And even the two who were too smart to be drawn into conversation by a . . . prisoner.

She turned her thoughts away from that thought, and daydreamed a bit about a world where everyone was kind to everyone else, and how these men would help bring it about . . . It seemed to her that both were needed: men of God to bring love; these men to guard against hate. She began to pray for them and their purpose—and before she knew it, the corporal looked out the window and said something and the seated guard got to his feet and looked alert; the guard at the door stepped aside. The door opened, and in with the warm air from outside came the chief of the San Juan police, Colonel Liebermann, who spoke both English and Spanish with a strong German-British accent; a short man in civilian clothes whom the soldiers saluted and called "Captain Bork"—and—Sister Bertrille's heart sank—Sister Plácido!

# *Nine*

The men got to their feet for the colonel and the
captain, Sister Bertrille got to her feet (and they
tingled!) for Sister Plácido, and they all stood; first
on one foot, then on the other, while the captain
looked at Sister Bertrille without looking at her; and
then he said to Sister Plácido, "This is *your* Sister
Bertrille? You identify her?"

Sister Plácido nodded, a stately, court nod that
took almost a minute from start to finish.

"Right," said the captain. And, to the San Juan
police chief: "You vouch for this ol—*this* Sister?"

Colonel Liebermann clicked his heels, bowed. "I
do."

The captain sat at Lieutenant Shannon's desk and
shoved the drawing aside without looking at it. He
seated them all with a glance and a gesture, then
said briskly, "I'm Captain Bork. There are a few
questions." He fixed cold blue eyes on Sister Bertrille. "What were you doing in there?"

Sister Bertrille quailed.

Colonel Liebermann said, "May I remind you,

sir, the lady is a civilian, therefore under my jurisdiction?"

Captain Bork slapped him with a glance. "Priority," he said, "*sir.* Priority." He turned on Sister. "Well?"

"It was an accident."

"Accident." The word went into a mental notebook. "How did you get in there?"

Sister sighed.

Sister Plácido nodded, the kind of nod that said, "Confess. *All.*"

Sister Bertrille said to the Counter-Intelligence man, "I flew."

That was obvious. He said, "Yes. In what?"

"Nothing," she said. "*I* flew."

Captain Bork glared at Lieutenant Shannon, who shrugged contentedly. It wasn't his problem any longer.

"Get the radarman here," Bork ordered.

The sergeant reached for the telephone.

"*How?*" Bork turned on Sister again.

"Behind some pelicans," she murmured, beginning to enjoy herself. She didn't like the captain. Oh, she didn't *dis*like him; she just didn't *like* him. The few words he said, he said from behind his hand, something to frustrate lip readers when he was out counterspying, no doubt, but it was twice as frustrating to someone he was questioning, when you couldn't be sure whether he had said, "How?" or, "Who?"

Colonel Liebermann gave her a nod that was an admonition—to do *what,* she didn't know—then he said in German-British to the captain, "*my* prisoner, sir."

Captain Bork threw the colonel an exasperated look. "What kind of report can I make out if I have to say that the prisoner flapped in behind some pelicans?"

Sister Plácido winced.

"Quite," said the colonel. "Shall we hear out the radarman?" He crossed his legs, released the precise crease of his trousers, rested one arm on the chair arm.

"Now, tell me, from the beginning," Bork said behind his hand.

He was looking at Sister Bertrille, so she told him—from the first bump at the corner to the final falling-leaf maneuver that had dropped her into the Security Area.

"I believe her," one of the guards said to the wall.

Corporal Page, the radarman, came in. He said that fifteen blips, pelicans by size and flight pattern, had shown on the screen; the last pelican had fallen, slipping, presumably to the ground.

"You *saw* it hit the ground?"

"No, sir. You know the radar doesn't register below—" He glanced at the Sisters, at Colonel Liebermann. Aware that this was classified information, he said, "Below a certain point."

"Yet you saw it fall."

"Yes, sir. She fell out of formation about sixty feet, did a fast sort of falling-leaf—"

"*She!* You could tell it was a she on the *radar?*"

"That was a figure of speech, sir, like ships are shes. But this blip was the same size as a pelican and flew in the same pattern. Planes come straight on, in a different kind of formation; this was a regular flight of pelicans, I'd swear to it, only they lost one. I thought one of the boys had got trigger happy—"

"That'll do." The Counter-Intelligence man was still in the army, and military-civilian relations weren't *that* good, that he'd allow the mention of shooting pelicans in front of the local police chief, who was supposed to protect the pelicans.

"You guarantee that the screen was under surveillance at all times?"

"Yes, sir."

"And nothing else showed up?"

"No, sir. Not for fifteen minutes before or after. It's logged."

"Witnesses?"

"Yes, sir. Smith, and Petrovsky."

"All right." He dismissed the radarman and said gently, respectfully, *too* respectfully, the way a reporter does when he's tempting someone to tell all, "Sister Bertrille, what makes you think you can fly?"

Sister felt helpless. He wouldn't believe her, why should he? She said hesitantly, "I could show you . . ."

Colonel Liebermann stood up. "I remind you, Captain, that this *civilian* prisoner—"

"All right," Captain Bork said. He looked tired.

The matter of principle and right having been established, Colonel Liebermann said generously, "If you should care to be the guest of the Insular Government—"

Captain Bork got to his feet. "I wouldn't miss it for the world."

Judge Torres' office was modern, clean, air-conditioned; Judge Torres himself was a craggy-faced Latin with dark eyes that listened, observed, made no comment. He sat at his desk with his hands folded, his pepper-and-salt hair neatly combed, his eyes waiting.

The two Sisters, the colonel and the captain sat in a semicircle facing him. Sister had just finished telling her story—again.

Judges Torres didn't move. He didn't say anything.

Sister didn't know what else to say. She didn't blame them for not believing her. And who did she have for a witness? Sister Sixto and Sister Plácido—but neither of them had actually seen her do anything but come in for some rather sloppy landings.

She said earnestly to the judge, "I've been reading up on flight and aerodynamics, and while it still seems improbable, it's not really impossible, when you consider that what I was doing was not actually flying, but *gliding*: unless the wind was very strong, and exactly in the right direction, I never got off the ground."

Judge Torres said gently, "Sor Bertrille, we here

are not attempting to decide *whether* you flew, or how—the point is that you have intruded upon a Security Area—unauthorized entry—which offense comes under the Espionage Act."

"*Espionage!* But all they asked was how I got in there," she protested. "And that was flying."

"That is what *they* wanted to know. But *we*, here, must decide whether or no you have committed a hostile act: espionage, attempted sabotage, that sort of thing."

"If she *does* fly," Colonel Liebermann suggested, "it might prove her veracity."

"In this instance," Captain Bork said.

Sister Plácido said firmly, "I attest to Sister Bertrille's absolute honesty, in all things."

Captain Bork stared at her and said from behind his hand, "Did she tell you she was bombing around nights with a bunch of pelicans?"

Sister Bertrille looked apology at Sister Plácido. "Not right away—but only because Sister had a heart attack last year, and she was so upset about my waving at sailors I thought she'd have another, and so there was no telling at all *what* would happen if—"

"You're the wackiest nun I ever heard of!" Captain Bork interrupted. "When were you waving at sailors?"

Judge Torres gave him a gavel-thump of a look. "We are not here considering Sister's other—er"—he seemed to have trouble finding something; his eyes twinkled, he looked as though he would laugh, then he frowned, rubbed his forehead, said in a choked voice, "activities."

Sister Bertrille said hastily, "It's only that I had never had this problem before. Where I come from, it isn't very windy—and when I found out I could fly, it was such a fantastic feeling that I got a little—uproarious about it."

"An uproarious nun," Captain Bork said.

"That wasn't the word I wanted, it was the only one I could think of at the moment."

"Right. But you're still the darnedest nun I ever heard of."

"Really," Sister Bertrille pleaded with him, "I didn't *mean* to do anything wrong! I wasn't *going* to go out last night, I was half asleep, and didn't even realize it wasn't a dream until we were out to sea."

Captain Bork's look said that it would be better for all of them if she had stayed at sea.

"I'd like to believe you," Judge Torres said.

Colonel Liebermann snapped to attention without getting out of his chair, a thing only Prussians can do. "*I* believe."

"I *can't!*" Captain Bork forgot to cover his mouth, he was so upset. It didn't matter, though, because he talked without moving his lips. "Washington isn't going to '*believe*'!"

Judge Torres said, "I don't think it's that serious. If we could just find a way to keep Sister on the ground—"

Bork worked up a scowl for an angry retort but,

at that moment, the door opened and the policeman on duty said to the judge, *Señor Juez, allí 'stá Don Scarpo de la Torre.*"

Judge Torres' somber face lighted up. He got to his feet to greet Don Scarpo, who looked the picture of humble helplessness. Don Scarpo bowed to the nuns, to the men, and stood, out of the element of his grocery store, looking with apology at the judge.

Sister Bertrille's heart went out to him, he looked so small.

Captain Bork ignored him after the first glance.

Don Scarpo said to Judge Torres in English, "Taked a while to find her." He nodded at Sister Plácido.

"I'm sorry I didn't call you right away," the judge said.

Don Scarpo deprecated that with flipping fingers. "It was not your place."

"Who's *this?*" Bork demanded.

The judge said, "Don Scarpo is the unofficial guardian angel of San Tanco. Whenever the Sisters need something, he mentions it about the city until they get it."

"Prejudiced witness," Bork muttered, like a man who knows he's going to be shouted down.

Colonel Liebermann knew better what would speak to Captain Bork. "Don Scarpo was one of Segarra's Rangers—the first company of the U. S. Rangers," he said.

Bork was outraged and at the same time de-

lighted. He pounced. "Don't give me that! *I* know
Darby had the first—"

"In the *1917* war," Colonel Liebermann said. "*I*
remember them—too well."

Judge Torres, taking the cue, added, "And in
World War II, it was Don Scarpo who—"

"Never mind, never mind." Bork, who hadn't
even been born in 1917, knew when he was licked.
"I accept his loyalty."

Judge Torres said to Don Scarpo, "Did you want
to say something?"

"Only this." Don Scarpo looked at Sister Bertrille,
who was obviously a prisoner, with a policeman
standing behind her chair, Bork on one side, Colonel
Liebermann on the other, both slightly to the rear
so they could observe her. "You flew into some-
place?" She nodded, and he said, "I knew. It had
to be." And to the judge: "I was seeing Sister flying
—several times. And when Sor Plácido was leaving
tonight with Colonel Liebermann, I didn't naturally
know *what* was the matter; but I suspected, yes,
that something was amissing, and so came I rapidly
to checking with allabody to see where was my
Sister Plácido and I came to finding you here.
And I am having to say only this: that this Sister
Bertrille is being as innocent as any newly being
born baby, for I was seeing the first flight she was
taking, and this was being purely by accident, by
the wind which was too muchly strong for her very
smallness. And she was being surprised, oh, yes, so
much! And so I am here by witnessing to her very

goodness of character which is excellent, superb for honesty."

Judge Torres and Colonel Liebermann were pleased, so pleased that they looked ready to congratulate Don Scarpo for his timely attestation.

But Bork was not. He said, in thinly veiled threat, for the whole United States was his to protect, and he had to do something, "What do you think the Federal Government's going to do to a local government that lets people pop into Security Areas and get away with it?"

Everyone sighed. He was being very difficult.

"What would convince you of her innocence?" Sister Plácido asked.

"I'd like to *see* her fly."

Judge Torres shuddered. "Not me."

"What else?" Colonel Liebermann asked.

"If a jury said she was innocent, I'd accept that. Or if she was committed—"

"Committed!" Judge Torres said very quietly. "Does this look an insane woman to you?"

"Look," Captain Bork said wearily, "all I know is, birds fly, bugs fly, planes fly. Not *people*." He sounded besieged. "Regulations won't let me consider her to be anything else but a spy or a nut."

Sister Plácido said to Judge Torres, "It has been decided that when I retire the Convent of San Tanco will be turned over to the jurisdiction of the American Province of our Order. Sister Bertrille was chosen and sent here as the most likely candidate for my successor."

Captain Bork looked as though he thought the Order must be chock-full of nuts.

Sister Bertrille got that cold feeling in her heels. Successor! What kind of superior could she make, flopping about in the sky after a bunch of pelicans? She began to feel some sympathy for Captain Bork.

She said to him, "What if I show you I can fly? What then?"

Colonel Liebermann said to Sister Plácido, "Excuse me, but how would one go about making a Sister Superior out of—" He indicated Sister Bertrille with a glance that was kindly, tolerant, incredulous; and a grin that was a silent burst of laughter.

"Sister Bertrille," said Sister Plácido, "has shown qualities of leadership, tact, adaptability, generosity, and holiness."

"A holy pelican," Bork muttered.

Sister Plácido ignored him. "We would nurture these qualities: Sister would be encouraged to discipline herself, to take on more and more responsibilities, until the time came that I should be allowed to spend out my days in rest and prayer and contemplation . . ."

Suddenly Sister Bertrille saw that Sister Plácido was a very old woman: an old woman who was holding herself together and tall by sheer power of will, holding herself and the Convent of San Tanco together until someone younger and stronger could relieve her of the burden of her duties. Sister Bertrille's eyes filled with tears, and she bowed her head.

"And all my foolishness destroyed your chance for peace."

Colonel Liebermann said, with a gentleness of voice that belied the ramrod stiffness of his attitude, "Once, when I was young, my brother and I made the groomsmen help us: we set up the farm wagon and four horses in the second-floor ballroom of our home—then we crept to bed. When our father came down in the morning—" He broke off, laughing.

Sister Bertrille tried to show interest in this kindly distraction, but her eyes bothered her. She patted them with her handkerchief.

Don Scarpo watched Captain Bork.

Captain Bork said, "What did he do?"

"Oh! He said that we had no right to endanger the lives of the groomsmen. So we two, alone, had to fetch down the wagon and the horses." Colonel Liebermann was laughing so hard he was red in the face. "You know that a horse will go willingly *up*stairs, but *down!* Oh, no, never!" He fingered a long crooked scar on his cheek that Sister had assumed was a saber scar: but now that she looked at it, it *could* have been made by a wagon tongue or a horse's hoof.

She said, disappointed, and only then realizing that she had hoped his story might mean something, "But that won't help Sister Plácido."

"Oh? No, of course not." He said gently, "I only told it to show that most young people of spirit do sometimes one strange thing in their life." He took the smile from his face, said in a cold voice, "And

then they grow up to be hardened old colonels of
police."

"Thank you," she said to the colonel, "but right
now I've lost all chance to be any help to Sister.
And Captain Bork"—she turned to him—"you must
know that, if I go on trial, that will be the end: I
couldn't even be a Sister any more—"

"Why would you want to be, if you can fly without a plane? You could make a fortune—"

"I don't want a fortune. My fortune is in San
Tanco—or wherever else I'm sent." She knew what
her fate would be when the Provincial heard about
this. And perhaps it was the only answer. She loved
San Juan, and San Tanco, and the Children and the
Old People there, but it wouldn't do them any good
to have an airborne Sister trying to take care of
them. And that first time she hadn't intended to
fly—and it *could* happen again—so she would be
sent away, to some quiet part of the country where
there wasn't much wind. Daughters of Charity don't
take permanent vows, but renew their vows each
year, so it would be no great scandal if she left
the convent—but for her it would be calamitous.
She didn't want to imagine any other life than this
she had in San Tanco: being useful, being needed,
being close to God in the life of prayer and love.
And all she had to do to remain a humble nun was
to convince one flat-footedly practical captain that
she meant her country no harm. But how?

To the German-born colonel and the Latin judge,
she was "only a woman," and therefore allowances

were made, as a matter of course. But to this captain —a woman was a competitor, an equal—and *this* woman, a menace to his country.

She said to him, "Please, listen: if I show you that I can fly, and I promise that I never will again—"

"Okay, okay!" The captain was a man battling unknown forces, but as long as they didn't threaten his country— "If it's all right with the judge and the colonel—and the ranger, here—I'd just as soon forget that I ever saw you."

Judge Torres put his hands on the edge of the desk, pressed down. "Sor Bertrille, how do you know when the wind is right for you to fly?"

"I don't, really. Just, when the pelicans came by from over Don Scarpo's store, then I knew, though I didn't *think* about it—it was a sort of intuitive knowledge." She sighed. "And when they called, I felt as though they were calling *me*."

Captain Bork said, "I remember, when the wild geese went over in the fall, how they seemed to be calling . . ." Then he snapped to attention. Because he was bewildered by his own reactions, he behaved angrily. "Oh, no you don't! You foreigners are trying to make a joke out of the United States, using this crackpot dame as a tool: and I'm not about to let you get away with it!" He was not a very big man, but he was a very clever man. He had not allowed himself any emotions for so long that now that he found himself with pity for the old and the young nuns, sympathy for the Prussian colonel and the Puerto Rican judge, he bent over backward to keep these emotions from influencing his judgment.

"Okay, Sister," he said. "You show me you can fly, *then* I'll let you know what I'll do. Not before." He glared at the others, whom he felt were aligned against him. And to Sister, "On your feet. Let's go."

Colonel Liebermann stood up and stepped delicately between them.

Judge Torres said, "I remind you, sir, Sister is a civilian—"

Sister said to Judge Torres, *"Please . . ."*; and to the colonel: "It means *so much . . ."* She knew they were strong men, wise men, good men, both of them; and that their wisdom and experience told them that this was an unwise solution. Solutions, for them, came of unemotional discussion, of long deliberation, of consultation with the books that held the wisdom of the ages. No problem, they *knew,* had ever been solved by a nun's leaping into flight.

Yet the younger man's threat of the Federal Government . . . Colonel Liebermann would remember another National Government; Judge Torres would remember when his island had been a territory and the Federal Government had been invoked by every unscrupulous trader.

They went along.

# *Ten*

They clustered at the foot of the flight of stairs
that led to the Sisters' floor at the top of the building. Sister Plácido stopped, her back to the stairs,
and looked at them pleadingly. The Rule did not
allow *anyone* but Sisters above, on that floor.

"Up there is the convent," she murmured, "no
externes . . ."

Colonel Liebermann, Judge Torres, and Don
Scarpo, delighted with the excuse, about-faced and
started back, but bumped into Captain Bork.

"I'll get a search warrant," he said. "Not from
you, but the FBI—"

Judge Torres' carefully shielded temper broke
into a thousand pieces. "Go ahead!" he snarled. "The
FBI agents here are named Murphy, Lopez, and
Nowak—and they're all Catholics!" He wasn't sure
that they were, but it was a pretty safe bet, with
names like that.

Bork began to look angry himself. He braced himself as though he were ready to go down fighting
all these foreigners for the U.S.A.

*"Please,"* Sister Bertrille said to the three who faced Bork, "it means *so much* . . ."

In the light from the single electric bulb over the stairs a three-inch cockroach buzzed, and Sister Plácido glanced up at it. She looked pale, and very tired, and *old*.

Sister Bertrille moved and put her foot on the first stair. The colonel and the judge and Don Scarpo stepped back to let Bork precede them, but he waved a hand as though it held a gun, and they went up, after the Sisters, before Bork.

They waited on the gallery while Sister Plácido routed Sister Narciso and Sisters Cook and Laundress out of bed and into another room; then they all went through the four-alcoved room and out onto the balcony.

It was four o'clock in the morning. Overhead the stars were thick in the black sky. The ebbing sea murmured at the base of the city wall, two hundred feet below. The breeze was tender, gentle.

Colonel Liebermann helped Sister Bertrille up onto the rail of the balcony, and tried to stay beside her, but Bork slid between them. Don Scarpo hitched himself up to sit on the rail, then, like a little boy riding a banister, he swung one leg over the rail, inched toward Sister. Bork halted him with that gun-waving gesture.

Sister lifted her arms over her head and looked down.

Three stories below, the cobblestones glistened darkly.

She looked up.

The millions of stars gleamed and glowed, but not one bird flew there in the night.

She was shaken with terror. She couldn't fly—not then, with no wind, when even the pelicans were asleep because the night wind had died— Besides, she never had *flown;* she had just been carried about by the wind.

She looked down at the five people on the balcony: Don Scarpo was watching Captain Bork; the colonel and the judge were edging closer, as close as Captain Bork would let them. Sister Plácido leaned—and she was no *leaner*—against the door jamb, one hand clutching it for support.

Judge Torres reached for her, said "Sister—*no!*"

She turned her face away, closed her eyes, clamped her teeth together, and pushed away from the wall.

She was wrenched violently, her feet caught on the rail, she grasped the shoulders of a coat, and an angry voice said, "I never *saw* such a fool thing!"

Captain Bork.

He hadn't been able to let her try. He had caught her and pulled her back to safety. She held to the shoulders of his coat for a second, then let go, feeling her feet firm on the balcony tiles.

"God bless you."

She turned to Sister Plácido, who reached out her hands, smiling—and fainted.

Sister Bertrille and Sister Sixto put Sister Plácido

to bed, and when the doctor had gone, saying that
it was exhaustion, and that they should let his pa-
tient get a good night's sleep some time, Sister Plácido closed her eyes, then opened them, and said,
"Sisters."

Sister Sixto and Sister Bertrille bent over her anx-
iously.

"Sister Bertrille."

"Yes, Sister." Sister Bertrille bent over the bed.

"See the gentlemen to the door."

Sister Bertrille, torn between laughter and tears,
said, "Yes, Sister."

"Sister Sixto."

Sister Sixto bent over the bed.

"You will chaperone Sister."

"Yes, Sister."

"Sister Bertrille."

"Yes, Sister?"

"You are in charge until"—her eyelids drooped;
she was a very tired old woman, who wanted only
a bit of rest, but also a strong old woman—"until
morning."

Downstairs the four men stood in the porte-co-
chère.

Sister Sixto and Sister Bertrille came to see them
to the door, where they were.

Don Scarpo said, "I have something for you, when
you come tomorrow."

"Thank you, Don Scarpo." He would have candy

for her children, or some Spanish delicacy for the old people.

He went out of there, a small, apologetic-looking little man.

A gold and scarlet dawn blazed across the sky. Captain Bork said to Judge Torres, "I'm sorry, sir, I interfered with your handling of your prisoner."

Judge Torres said to Sister, and he was smiling, a broad, white smile in his dark face, "How now do you feel about flying?"

She said humbly, "There'll be no more of that." And knew that it was true. She'd manage, somehow.

Colonel Liebermann said, "I think she will grow up to be a very fine colonel of police."

"One with a *heart*," Sister said to him.

Judge Torres laughed. "Well then, I remand you to your own custody. And I believe that, for the good of all concerned, the record of this hearing should be—"

"Who made a record?" Captain Bork said.

Sister said to him, "God bless you—and thank you—I'll never forget you."

"All I want is to forget you," he assured her.

Then they were gone, Sister Bertrille and Sister Sixto went upstairs, and the convent slept for another half hour. The next afternoon Sister Bertrille was sent across the street to Don Scarpo's for some saffron.

He said gently, "You look tired, my Sister."

She didn't mention the night, said only, "The wind—it blows me about so, Don Scarpo."

He smoothed down his mustache and said, "Oh, yes. I have something for you." He whirled around, back again, and set a handful of fishing weights upon the counter.

Every nun as she walks along makes a faint click-click, the sound of her rosary beads. But Sister Bertrille, as she walks along, makes a clickety-click-click-clickety—the sound of her rosary and three dozen eight-ounce lead fishing weights sewn inside the hem of her habit.

Anyone knows that eighteen pounds of fishing weights would make her weigh ninety-three pounds. And everyone knows that a ninety-three-pound nun can't fly.

# Charity Sisters Changing Habit

The Daughters of Charity of Saint Vincent de Paul announced this week that the order will make its first change of habit in three hundred years.

Beginning September 20, according to Sister Eleanor, Provincial of the Eastern Province of the Daughters of Charity in the United States, sisters of the order will wear a one-piece, box pleated, tailored dress with a hemline six inches from the floor.

The new headdress is white, covered by a short blue coiffe reaching below the shoulders. The color of the habits will remain blue and white to indicate the order's special dedication to Mary Immaculate.

The present habit, with its large stiffly starched headpiece or "cornette" is modeled after the costume of the Normandy peasant woman of the 17th century.

The change of habit was made in compliance with recommendations from the Sacred Congregation of Religious in Rome which has urged that religious orders of women simplify their habits in keeping with the needs of their present work and with the general trend of adaption to modern times.

To the community, the largest in the Catholic Church, with more than 45,000 members in 5 continents, 65 countries and 52 Provinces, the change posed several problems. Because of the variety of activities in which the sisters engage, the new habit had to be trim, simple and suitable for all weather service.

From the Generalate in Paris, the Superioress General sent word to all of the Provincials throughout the world, inviting suggestions for the new habit. After careful studies and international consultations, the new design was approved.

The American Sisters of Charity, founded by Blessed Elizabeth Ann Seton in 1809, wore the black habit and bonnet of their foundress until 1850 when they became affiliated with the French Daughters of Charity of St. Vincent de Paul and adopted the cornette and blue habit.

Works of the order include practically everything that active orders of women do: in hospitals, both general and special; schools from kindergarten through college; homes for dependent children and for the aging; home nursing; Catechetics; social welfare, care and counseling of unwed mothers; mobile dispensaries; hostels, day camps and youth centers.

Much of the Sister's work, though institution-based, is done outside of the institution in both urban and rural areas.

Reprinted from *Baltimore Catholic Review,* August 14, 1964

Do you suppose the published reason is the *real* reason?

## Advisory Corps Staff

| | |
|---|---|
| Command & Tra-<br>jectory | Col. Page Smith |
| Insecurity | Lieut. James A. Linen |
| Weaponry, Judo &<br>Karate | Stephen V. Versace |
| Disorientation | Col. & Mrs. James W. Chapman |
| Raised Eyebrows | James F. Cassin |
| Care & Feeding of<br>Nuns & Habits | Lolly Quarantillo |
| Good Grammaritan | Kathy Dewey |
| RCP Law & Order | Elaine Prather |
| PI & Empaginando | Mike & Tracy Versace |
| Morale | Rev. William B. Faherty, S.J. |
| Character<br>Guidance | Ch. (Lt. Col.) Aloysius<br>Bertrand<br>Ch. (Capt.) Joseph Nosser |
| Sine Quo Non | Dick Prazych |